Learning the Prophetic

"Arise, shine, for your light has come,
and the glory of the Lord rises upon you.
See, darkness covers the earth
and thick darkness is over the peoples,
but the Lord rises upon you
and his glory appears over you.
Nations will come to your light,
and kings to the brightness of your dawn."

\- Isaiah 60:1-3

AF372938

Leroy D. Fearon

Leroy D. Fearon

Copyright © 2019 Leroy D. Fearon

All rights reserved.

ISBN-13: 978-9768277510

All rights reserved

Unless otherwise noted, all scripture references are taken from the New International version of the Holy Bible.

For more information or to place an order. please contact:

Leroy D. Fearon

Email: leroyfearon85@gmail.com

Leroy D. Fearon

DEDICATION

I dedicate this book to my parents, Ann-Marie and Leroy Fearon, whom I love wholeheartedly.

You've always been my heroes. You've always been my pride; you've always given so much love and shown what's deep inside. You are everything I could ever need and more. You love God and, so, you could love me. You've sacrificed your whole life's work for me so I could soar.

You've lived every principle you taught me and that's what I admire the most. I pray that God will bless you with longevity so you can continue to watch me skyrocket into the prophetic and share my journey with you and the world.

- Your son.

CONTENTS

ACKNOWLEDGEMENTS

I want to acknowledge the King of Kings and the Lord of Lords, Jesus Christ, the Son of the Most High God, for birthing this book in my spirit. My life will never be the same again as I advance in the knowledge of God. You have answered many prayers and, have indeed, fulfilled your promise to me, your son.

Sincere gratitude to my family who gave me space to obediently record this manuscript as I was inspired by the Holy Spirit.

I also want to express thanks to a friend, Mrs. Beckford, whom God has allowed to assist me with the preparation and publication of this book. She has also been an inspiration as an author, preacher and teacher of the Word.

To my editors, Mr. Kirkton Bennett and Mrs. Shakera Hanson-Powell (Language Specialists), with their keenness, who ensured that the script was expertly vetted

Ms. Kadian Spencer who has been of tremendous support to me in my spiritual walk, thank you servant of God.

And finally, but by no means the least, Ms. Dacia Green (University IT Major} for her expertise in designing my cover almost exactly the way I saw it in my spirit. My deepest gratitude to you.

INTRODUCTION

You have picked up a copy of "Learning the Prophetic" by Leroy D. Fearon. The miracle enclosed in the form of this book is a demonstration of the infinite possibilities when you live a life devoted to Christ.

This prophetic literature was born out of the author's devotion on New Year's Day 2019. The Lord gave specific instructions pertaining to the title for the chapters and a vivid description of the book. In obedience, the author penned the revelation and the Lord placed the parties together so that this life-changing book, filled with many insightful experiences in the prophetic, can be shared to edify prophetic people, Christians, church leaders and people who desire to be equipped with knowledge to prevent deception in the last days.

There are many who have smothered their prophetic gift, experiences and dreams but with renewed strength, boldness and knowledge from the contents of this book, you will be released by the Holy Spirit to grow, rise and stand in your purpose and advance the kingdom of God on earth.

Chapter One

Who is a Prophet?

This is a question many people ask in today. Many people are called prophets simply because they are filled with the Holy Spirit or maybe because they possess deep discernment, a gift of the spirit or because they conduct themselves in a Christ-like manner. Being a prophet, however, is far from these assumptions. In order to shape a definition of a prophet, I have analyzed the prophets of old, since they were the 'original' prophets and the prophets God mentioned time and time again in His Scriptures.

The word 'prophet' in itself denotes a male character. Therefore, based on Scripture any man who has been called by God to speak on behalf of Him to a people, nation or tribe concerning their lifestyle (religious practices, conduct, speech, rebellion in any way just to name a few) can be referred to as a prophet. In addition, this person would portray a number of characteristics based on the Bible. A prophetess would, therefore, be their female counterpart. *For example*: Anna daughter of Phanuel, of the tribe of Asher (Luke 2:36).

Characteristics/Qualities of a True Prophet

Based on my knowledge of the prophetic, these are some common qualities you will and should identify in those who claim to be prophetic vessels, are known as prophets or even consecrated to the Office of the Prophet:

1. All true prophets by the nature of their work in the kingdom must have the gift of prophecy.

2. All true prophets possess the fruit of the spirit (all prophets must possess the by-products of living for God—love, joy, peace, patience, kindness, goodness, faithfulness, gentleness and self-control (Gal. 5:22-23).

3. All true prophets acknowledge that Jesus is Lord. (1 John 4:2 "This is how you can recognize the spirit of God: Every spirit that acknowledges that Jesus Christ has come in the flesh is from God.")

4. All true prophets are reliable and people can trust that what they speak are the words of God (1 Samuel 3: 19).

5. All true prophets have a mind to build and not to tear down God's people, or works with godly intentions (Neh. 2:11-20; Neh. Ch. 3 & 4).

The qualities are extensive and not limited to only these above. The ones highlighted above are simply the most obvious or should be the most obvious.

It is important to note that some prophets tried to turn people back to God; for example: Jonah. Others may predict the future as revealed by God. A prophet's role is to preach God's word to the people—warning, instructing and encouraging them to live as they ought.

How Do I Know I am Called to the Prophetic?

Firstly, I would say, any gifting you are particularly drawn to usually is your area. Personally, I never fit in. My spiritual experiences are usually outside of the norm; which I thought were the experiences of every spirit-filled believer.

Unfortunately, this was not the case. I found that I was keen on the intricacies in my dreams, interpreting emotions and tones…and my 'predictions' of what was happening in a person's life were usually accurate. In addition, I was also able to see future events. This is also a clear indicator that you are prophetic, especially if your experiences are frequent. Furthermore, what I noticed was that I have a deeper discernment, especially when the prophetic anointing is resting on me heavily (as I flow in other areas too by God's grace). For example, I remember a few years ago when I stood to moderate in a Youth Sunday service at a local church. I delayed to speak for a few seconds because I wanted to follow the leading of God's Spirit and not necessarily by what I had on paper. Then suddenly I heard the voice of an elder. I was shocked because the mouth of the individual was closed. I was not certain but I was curious that it was the Spirit of God. When I went home after the church service, I prayed to God concerning the matter and I asked Him to prove to me again that I was actually discerning the thoughts of the person. The second time, I heard the voice of the same person and, this time for sure, the individual's mouth was closed and this was proof enough that God can do anything if we are open and available. The thoughts I heard the second time made me re-think, and I was a little shaken and taken aback because I did not expect that from such an individual. The Bible made no mistake when it emphasized "…the heart instead of the outward man", referenced in 1 Sam. 16: 7: "But the Lord said to Samuel, "Do not look at his appearance or at his physical stature, because I have refused him. For the Lord does not see as man sees; for man looks at the outward appearance, but the Lord looks at the heart". Amen.

If you have spoken as you are led by the Spirit of God to speak concerning events, if God has so impressed on your heart to speak to an obstinate people, perhaps it may be your local church; if you have been operating outside of the norm and possess these qualities, you may very well be prophetic. You may be anointed with the gift of prophecy or you may be called to the Office of the Prophet (which we will discuss to a greater extent in a future chapter).

Gifts that Flow with the Gift of prophecy or When You are Called to the Office of the Prophet

"To one there is given through the *Spirit a*

message of wisdom, to another a message of knowledge by means of the same Spirit, to another faith by the same Spirit, to another gifts of healing by that one Spirit, to another miraculous powers, to another prophecy, to another distinguishing between spirits, to another speaking in different kinds of tongues, and to still another the interpretation of tongues" —1 Corinthians 12: 8-10.

Here, this, is a reminder of the gifts of the Spirit. in case you have forgotten them. Being filled with the Spirit does not limit you because we serve a limitless God; a God who can do exceedingly abundantly above all we can ask or think (Eph. 3: 20-21). This, therefore, means as a believer, God can allow you to flow in any gift He sees fit. This, however, does not negate the fact that prophetic people would have a specific calling on their lives.

Hence, they will 'specialize' in a particular gift or gifting if I may say it this way. For example, I am prophetic but I also possess a unique ability to preach and teach the word of God. I am as experienced in those areas as I am experienced in the prophetic. Without boast, I believe I was heavily graced. Thank you, Jesus.

In relation to the sub-heading, based on my experiences in the prophetic, a person with the gift of prophecy would have **wisdom** simply because God speaks to them via His Spirit. Therefore, they tend to know what is ahead. Amos 3:7 says, "Surely the Sovereign LORD does nothing without revealing his plan to His servants the prophets." In addition, discerning of spirit/knowledge. In 2 Kings 5: 25-26, it was clear that the **gift of discernment** is strong among prophets. When he went in and stood before his master, Elisha asked him, "Where have you been, Gehazi?"

"Your servant didn't go anywhere," Gehazi answered. But Elisha said to him, "Was not my Spirit with you when the man got down from his chariot to meet you? Is this the time to take money or to accept clothes—or olive groves and vineyards, or flocks and herds, or male and female slaves? Naaman's leprosy will cling to you and to your descendants forever."

Then Gehazi went from Elisha's presence and his skin was leprous—it had become as white as snow. The prophet of the Most High God was able to discern the falsehood and confront it. The servant might have been shocked that the prophet was able to prove that he lied but the Bible outlined no indication of such. This, however, highlights a prophet's insight as God enables them.

Furthermore, all prophets I have met so far have the **gift of tongues** (although this is no prescribed requirement). They often speak as the spirit gave them utterance. As a young prophet, I have the gift of tongues. This is evidenced by the fact that at any given time my tongues will change. I often observe myself closely, it is usually a combination of different tongues. I am a lover of modern languages, as a result, I can readily identify when my tongues change. Usually, whenever the Lord gives me a fresh touch or a 'double portion' then my tongues would normally change.

Also, I would notice that while delivering a prophetic word whether to the local church body or one-to-one prophecies I would hear God speak but when I open my mouth it would be in tongues and then I would immediately interpret the tongues because the aim of the gift of prophecy is to edify. This is the major distinction between the gift of tongues and the gift of prophecy. The Apostle Paul wrote in 1 Corinthians 14:2-5 "For anyone who speaks in a tongue does not speak to people but to God. Indeed, no one understands them; they utter mysteries by the Spirit. But the one who prophesies speaks to people for their strengthening, encouraging and comfort. Anyone who speaks in a tongue edifies themselves, but the one who prophesies edifies the church. I would like every one of you to speak in tongues, but I would rather have you prophesy. The one who prophesies is greater than the one who speaks in tongues, unless someone interprets, so that the church may be edified."

Again, Spirit-filled believers can flow in any gift as the Lord desires but more so the ones highlighted and explained. I remember once in church and I experienced something I have never again experienced in my entire lifetime. I was in church worshipping and then it was as if my hands were on fire (I am trying to convey the experience into words) but not a burning kind. It felt like it was being washed but I knew by the Spirit that my hands were being purified.

Then the Lord told me to go and place my hand on a lady because she was sick. At the time my knowledge in the prophetic was limited and when I looked across the congregation the lady looked fine to me. Therefore, in my mind it was crazy. I disobeyed the Lord. Later that week about the Friday I was in dialogue with the person that God had spoken to me concerning. My fellow sister in Christ reported that she was hospitalized. Immediately, I knew it had something to do with my disobedience so I immediately contacted someone whom I could trust to share the experience and friend told me that they were almost at my house on their way to visit the church sister who was hospitalized.

I was encouraged to accompany the team and release God's healing on His servant. I went with the team and prayed and did as the Lord instructed me. Not long after the individual was healed. I sensed that healing was taking place as I felt some of the pains the individual experienced. When the church sister was fully recovered I confessed my disobedience although this could not have changed the fact that the sister also had a miscarriage while being hospitalized. "Obedience is better than sacrifice" (1 Sam 15:22}. I must also say there is no greater feeling than being obedient to God.

The Lord sent someone with a word to me that I believe will change my life and I hope it will change yours too. This minister said to me, "The Lord says whenever you disobey me, people are going to suffer" If my memory serves me right this was after the experience with the hospitalized woman. I struggled with disobedience simply because I was afraid of disrupting services or afraid of saying or doing what the Lord instructed me to do being that I was in unfamiliar territory and also this whole learning the voice of God experience was new for me; also, the presence of the prophetic was also new among the people. I did not want to start or engage in any form of conflict among the brethren.

I outlined all of this to bring to the fore that if you are prophetic, to be safe, try as best as is possible to walk in total obedience at all times. I certainly have failed at this many times but I am trying. We are one body in Christ and so as we are connected, our roles and functions influence each other, so does our obedience to our Father in heaven. Some people's deliverance is locked up inside of us, some people's healing is locked up inside of us, some people's encouragement is locked on the inside of us and until we obey, others will not be able to live victorious overcoming lives. Thank you, Jesus.

PRAYER

Please pray this Holy Ghost-inspired prayer for victory over disobedience:

Lord, You are Great! What is man that You are mindful of us? You are high and lifted up, You are our strength. Lord, I ask that You will forgive us for the many times we have disobeyed You, the many times we have allowed others to experience dark valleys and desolate times simply because we neglect Your leading, simply because we are prideful, simply because we undermine Your thoughts. But, Lord, we stand resolute that Your thoughts are higher and deeper than ours. By Your Spirit's power, help us to walk in total submission, in total obedience so that Your work can be accomplished on earth as it is in heaven. Please hear and answer, in Jesus' Name. Thank you, Lord.

Levels/Dimensions in the Prophetic

It must be a common understanding among believers

or Christians that not everyone will be called to the office of the prophet as well as the fact that not all prophetic people were predestined to be prophets. I agree with many writers and scholars that there are three dimensions or levels of the prophetic, as I have seen the manifestation of all three. They are as follows:

- ***The Spirit of Prophecy*-** This is where any spirit-filled believer can speak or prophesy on behalf of God. In my experience, this usually happens when the atmosphere is ripe, that is, the hearts of believers are at a place where they can commune with the place, at a place of penitence. I mostly see the spirit of prophecy poured on random believers in or after a rich worship experience. The message is usually one of exhortation.

- ***The Gift of Prophecy***- Persons on whom the gift was bestowed usually have an intimate relationship with God, they spend quality time in prayer and reading of God's word. These persons generally have to be able to discern the voice of God as they are usually used as God's vessel more frequently. These messages usually go beyond exhortation and can include giving a word of warning or correction to a local congregation.

- ***The Office of the Prophet***- Persons whom God has called to the Office of the prophet know exactly who they are as they directly receive messages from God. They have the mind of God and as such at any given time with the Spirit's permission they can share a deep revelation from the Lord. Persons whom

God has so anointed usually experience great miracles, supernatural experiences, and frequent visions depending on the type of prophet they are. These individuals possess deep discernment and can even finish your sentences for you. These individuals are exposed to so much activity in the spiritual realm that humility must be their daily food. These believers usually speak on God's behalf to a wider audience such as a nation or government. This was evident with the Major Prophets in the Bible.

THE F.A.A.M *will help you identify the category you fall into so you can be more useful to God in your capacity.*

The table below was developed based on my personal experiences in the prophetic. I call it the FAAM of the prophetic.

Criteria	Spirit of Prophecy	Gift of prophecy	Office of the Prophet
Frequency	Infrequent	Average (as the Lord see fit)	Very often
Audience	Tend to be smaller	Can be small or medium or even large depending on who the vessel is and their sphere of influence.	Wider scale due to their track record (reliability).

Accuracy	People in this category often have challenges delivering the word.	With experience they can be more accurate - younger prophets tend to omit some of the message so accuracy is swayed.	Very accurate due to experience and training of their gift.
Message	Simple exhortation	Warning and encouragement	Major warnings, Predicts major events/ gives major warnings

			to turn from sin etc.

Is it Possible to Move from One Category to the Next?

Yes! Every prophet must go through the process. It takes training of the gift. This is therefore connected to your obedience. If you are willing to obey then you grow faster through the various dimensions. Firstly, I experienced the spirit of prophecy in a rich worship atmosphere. It was unlike anything I had experienced at the time. I knew at the time the Lord used me to also do sign language as I spoke and was carried by the Spirit; I knew it was God as I was not trained then, in Sign Language. Then I transitioned to the gift, so I got some experience in speaking prophetically to an entire congregation on several occasions and this usually follows a rich worship experience. I believe I am the final stage which is the office of the prophet but in a junior category because there are still many things I need to learn. It's a working progress.

I see where God has been using me on a wider scale to impact lives. However, if it is not God's will for you to be a prophet then what I suggest is that you remain humble and seek His face so that whenever you minister you share from a place of boldness, purity, love and with accuracy as this is really what is important and not the title per se.

CHAPTER TWO

Growing in the Prophetic

The prophetic is delicate and, as such, it takes practice and more practice. Think of the prophetic as a new technical job; it will require you to do a few hands-on and over time you will get better. The same is true with the prophetic gift. In order to grow in your gifting and call measures must be taken. In order for one to grow physically, they must eat, that maintains proper nutrition.

With spiritual health it is similar. It is important to note that anyone who has the gift of prophecy or is in the office of the Prophet, that is, your call has been recognized by your church and those you influence then it simply means you are no longer an immature Christian. The fact that one can avail themselves to be used of and by God suggests some level of maturity; If you obey God then you are certainly closer to being the mature Christian God expects us to be.

Look at the Hebrew writer's discourse in warning the saints against falling away in Hebrews 5:12-14: "In fact, though by this time you ought to be teachers, you need someone to teach you the elementary truths of God's word all over again. You need milk, not solid food! Anyone who lives on milk, being still an infant, is not acquainted with the teaching about righteousness. But solid food is for the mature, who by constant use have trained themselves to distinguish good from evil".

Therefore, being a prophet is far from being immature. The Jewish Christians were immature.

Some of them should have been teaching others, but they had not even applied the basics to their own lives. They were reluctant to move beyond age-old traditions, established doctrines, and discussion of the basics. They would not have been able to understand the high- priestly role of Christ unless they moved out of their comfortable position, cut some of their Jewish ties, and stopped trying to blend in with their culture.

Commitment to Christ moves people out of their comfort zones. Commitment to the prophetic will move you outside of your comfort zone and force you to place your trust in Christ. I have been instructed by the Lord to do things that seemed crazy but I am reminded by His word that he "chose the foolish things of the world to shame the wise" (1 Cor. 1: 27).

In order to grow in the prophetic these were some of the measures undertaken:

1. ***Prophetic company*** - The Old Testament often speaks of the company of the prophets or school of the prophets. This as the concept suggests would be a group or community of prophetic voices working in tandem so that God's will be done. 1 Sam. 10:5-6 "After that you will go to Gibeah of God, where there is a Philistine outpost. As you approach the town, you will meet a procession of prophets coming down from the high place with lyres, timbrels, pipes, and harps being played before them, and they will be prophesying.

The Spirit of the Lord will come powerfully upon you, and you will prophesy with them, and you will be changed into a different person. Please note that when you are in the company of prophets the spirit of prophecy can fall on you. My first experience in the prophetic was among prophetic people so I know this to be true. Also, since I am on this point, may I also mention that prophetic people are connected? A prophet is usually able to discern when the Lord is about to speak through a vessel. This has also been my experience because, for some reason, I feel as if the word will be spoken through me. When in the company of prophets, God can also divide the 'work' and 'word' among the vessels if he sees fit for varied reasons.

I have also experienced this first hand. You might be saying how could Saul be so filled with the Spirit yet later commit such evil acts? Throughout the Old Testament, God's Spirit "came upon" a person temporarily so that God could use him or her for great acts. This happened frequently to Israel's judges when they were called by God to rescue the nation (Judges 3: 8-10). This was not always a permanent abiding influence, but sometimes a temporary manifestation of the Holy Spirit. Yet, at times in the Old Testament, the spirit came upon unbelievers to enable them to do unusual tasks (Numbers 24; 2 Chron 36:22, 23). The Holy Spirit gave the person power to do what God asked, but it did not always produce the other fruits of the Spirit, such as self-control. Saul in his early years as King was a different person (10:1-10) as a result of the Holy Spirit's work in him. But as Saul's power grew, so did his pride. After a while he refused to seek God; the Spirit left him (16:14); and his good attitude melted away.

Personally, I know that the company of the prophets helps any young prophet a great deal. I found that it was rather challenging to express myself to non-prophetic people, they had challenges understanding my experiences. I found that people who had a similar anointing and call on their lives related to me better and so, naturally I felt comfortable in their company. They encouraged me on several occasions so I knew I was not going crazy.

They helped me understand my many dreams as well as things the Lord had shown me in the Spiritual realms. I am forever grateful.

2. ***Invest in prophetic education*** - In order to grow in the prophetic, you must be enthused about it. In order for a doctor to learn about the body and care for it, they must be enthused about the workings of the body and seek to discover new knowledge. Prov. 19:2 "Desire without knowledge is not good-how much more will hasty feet miss the way". In other

words, zeal without knowledge is not good. Many plunge into jobs without evaluating whether or not they are suitable for the job. Never rush into the unknown. Be sure you understand what you are getting yourself into and where you want to go before you take the first step and if it still feels unknown, ensure you are following God.

On this premise, as I continued to experience the working of the prophetic in my life, I did many research, did many readings and listened to many experts and spoke to many prophetic people in my sphere of reach. The closer I got to them, the more I recognized that my experiences were normal and were not as a result of any birth or mental defect. Therefore, for me investing in prophetic education encompassed spending time in the prophetic company. Also, investing in prophetic education could also mean spending time with a mature prophet. Look at Elijah and Elisha in 2 Kings 2. Elisha knew who his master or teacher Elijah was. He was determined to be like him so everywhere Elijah went, Elisha would follow him even if Elijah had told him to stay. He was determined to learn, determined to walk the path of his predecessor. This is the kind of attitude we ought to have towards learning the things of God-a determination, comes what may, a determination that knows no bounds, no distance.

As a result, Elisha as an effective replacement for Elijah as God's prophet to Israel. Elisha had a great example to follow in the prophet Elijah. He remained with Elijah until the last moments of his teacher's life on earth. He was willing to follow and learn in order to gain the power to do the work to which God had called him. ***Investing in prophetic***

education will better guide our prophetic desires.

Look at Elisha's request in 2 Kings 2: 9-10: "When they had crossed, Elijah said to Elisha, "Tell me, what can I do for you before I am taken from you?" "Let me inherit a double portion of your spirit," Elisha replied. "You have asked a difficult thing," Elijah said, "yet if you see me when I am taken from you, it will be yours—otherwise, it will not" and by verses 13-15 of the same chapter, moments later, his request was made manifest. V. 13 Elisha then picked up Elijah's cloak that had fallen from him and went back and stood on the bank of the Jordan. He took the cloak that had fallen from Elijah and struck the water with it, v. 14. "Where now is the LORD, the God of Elijah?" he asked. When he struck the water, it divided to the right and to the left, and he crossed over. V. 15 The company of the prophets from

Jericho, who were watching, said, "The spirit of Elijah is resting on Elisha." And they went to meet him and bowed to the ground before him.

3. ***Get in the Word*** - Spend time in the Word of God and assessing the lives of the prophets in scripture and examine how they operated. I was keen to assess their individual weaknesses so that I do not make the same mistakes they did. I would have also looked at their strengths and they were all in-line with Christ-like character. Prophetic voices usually have a passion for God's intimacy. We must understand as saints that the surest form of prophecy is the word of God. Hallelujah. In order for prophets to have 'a word or a message' they must consume the word. In John 1:1 Says " In the beginning was the Word, and the Word was with God, and the Word was God." ***Therefore, if you have God living on the inside of***

you then you will always have a word, so to speak. A prophet must be able to identify the word of God. The scripture is God's word, inspired by his Spirit, in other words written by man under the inspiration of the Holy Spirit so it is safe to say it was written by God; so if you want to know God more, then read his word, If you want to learn His voice and His ways, read his word.

In summary, growing in the prophetic requires prophetic association (company), investment in prophetic education and knowledge of the word of God. If you are called to the prophetic too, then these might help you. If you are not called to the prophetic but you have the prophetic association, you will notice these traits in your friends, prophetic family members, and church leaders among others.

CHAPTER THREE

The Lifestyle of a Prophet

The lifestyles of prophets will differ. Lifestyle is relative as prophets or prophetic people can be found in different parts of the world and different cultures; as well as from varied socio-economic backgrounds. All these may somehow influence a prophet's lifestyle. However, living the life of a prophet is something God himself will teach you. In one of my most recent encounters with God, He told me He was going to teach me and I should use the anointing he has given me. Then I reflect on 1 John 2: 27 "As for you, the anointing you received from him remains in you, and you do not need anyone to teach you. But as his anointing teaches you about all things and as that anointing is real, not counterfeit-just as it has taught you, remain in him." This suggests we should put our trust in the Lord Jesus Christ to lead us and be open to His teaching through His word and His Spirit. God will do whatever is necessary to make us vessels worthy of His use if we avail ourselves. Therefore, do not think you will wear a garment of hair like Elijah or camel's hair with a leather belt like John; because we live in a totally different time period. ***What will remain constant in our lifestyle is holiness***.

CHAPTER THREE

The Lifestyle of a Prophet

The lifestyles of prophets will differ. Lifestyle is relative as prophets or prophetic people can be found in different parts of the world and different cultures; as well as from varied socio-economic backgrounds. All these may somehow influence a prophet's lifestyle. However, living the life of a prophet is something God himself will teach you. In one of my most recent encounters with God, He told me He was going to teach me and I should use the anointing he has given me. Then I reflect on 1 John 2: 27: "As for you, the anointing you received from him remains in you, and you do not need anyone to teach you. But as his anointing teaches you about all things and as that anointing is real, not counterfeit-just as it has taught you, remain in him." This suggests we should put our trust in the Lord Jesus Christ to lead us and be open to His teaching through His word and His Spirit. God will do whatever is necessary to make us vessels worthy of His use if we avail ourselves. Therefore, do not think you will wear a garment of hair like Elijah or camel's hair with a leather belt like John; because we live in a totally different time period. ***What will remain constant in our lifestyle is holiness***.

Another example of God's teaching was in Jeremiah 1 when the Lord called the prophet. In this case, it was not necessarily on how to live but how to carry out his duty (how to deliver the message). The Prophet Jeremiah said in Jer. 1: 6-8: "Alas, Sovereign Lord," I said, "I do not know how to speak; I am too young." But the Lord said to me, "Do not say, 'I am too young'. You must go to everyone I send you to and say whatever I command you. Do not be afraid of them, for I am with you and will rescue you," declares the Lord. Often people struggle with new challenges because they lack self-confidence, feeling that they have inadequate training, ability or experience.

Jeremiah thought he was "only a child"—too young and inexperienced to be God's spokesman to the world. But God promised to be with him. God will do the same for His prophets today. We should not allow feelings of inadequacy to keep us from obeying God's call. He will always be with us. ***When you find yourself avoiding something you know you should do, be careful not to use lack of self-confidence as an excuse. If God gives you a job to do, he will provide all you need to do it.***

Honesty is an important attribute in the life of a prophet. In the same text, Jeremiah 1, I realized that Jeremiah was honest. He was able to tell God at least what he thought would have prevented him from being ineffective and so God rectified it.

The lifestyle of any prophet would encompass the activities they engage themselves in that enables them to grow. If we look at prophets in the Bible, they were all given to prayer. Prayer is the lifeline of any prophet. Since we are using Jeremiah, this prophet ***walks with the Lord*** as all prophets should. In v. 8, Jeremiah did not have to ask God to walk with him but rather the Lord told him He would "be with him and rescue him". This is the reassurance we have not just as prophets and prophetic people but children of the Most High God; we have that promise. Therefore as a prophet or child of the King, God promised to rescue us from trouble, not to keep trouble from coming. God did not insulate Jeremiah from imprisonment, deportation, or insults. God does not keep us from encountering life's storms, but he will see us through them. In fact, God walks through these storms with us and rescues us.

Prophets endure **hardships** - True servants of God will suffer on account of Christ. Paul shared some of his sufferings in 2 Cor. 11:23-29 "Are they servants of Christ? (I am out of my mind to talk like this.) I am more. I have worked much harder, been in prison more frequently, been flogged more severely, and been exposed to death again and again. Five times I received from the Jews the forty lashes minus one. Three times I was beaten with rods, once I was pelted with stones, three times I was shipwrecked, I spent a night and a day in the open sea, I have been constantly on the move. I have been in danger from rivers, in danger from bandits, in danger from my fellow Jews, in danger from Gentiles; in danger in the city, in danger in the country, in danger at sea; and in danger from false believers.

I have labored and toiled and have often gone without sleep; I have known hunger and thirst and have often gone without food; I have been cold and naked. Besides everything else, I face daily the pressure of my concern for all the churches. Who is weak, and I do not feel weak? Who is led into sin, and I do not inwardly burn?" These hardships outlined are not just limited to prophets but just about any servant of God and to a greater extent, those who serve in leadership, Apostles and Pastors.

Like the prophets, the Apostle Paul not only

did Paul face beatings and dangers, he also carried the daily concern for the young churches, worrying that they were staying true to the gospel and free from false teachings and inner strife. Paul was concerned for individuals in the churches he served.

If God has placed you in a place of leadership and authority, treat people with Paul's kind of empathy and concern. Prophets always seem to take on the burden of others and so in turn burden themselves by standing in the gap for people who sometimes in turn disregard God's grace. Moses was a prime example of such.

As saints in Christ, we must always be mindful of the fact that long suffering is a fruit of the spirit so true servants of God will have to endure it. These are necessary to "tip the balance'. Without these necessary struggles, we will forget God and/or take his glory for self.

As a result, this will lead to self-destruction and ultimately eternal damnation if one refuses to repent.

CHAPTER FOUR

Prophesying to a People You Know

Prophesying to a people you know is never easy. Sharing a word whether preaching, teaching or exhortation, it is never easy when done in the presence of your own. In John Mark's account in Mark 6: 1-4, it is stated that: "Jesus left there and went to his hometown, accompanied by his disciples. When the Sabbath came, he began to teach in the synagogue, and many who heard him were amazed. "Where did this man get these things?" they asked. "What's this wisdom that has been given him? What are these remarkable miracles he is performing? Isn't this the carpenter? Isn't this Mary's son and the brother of James, Joseph, Judas, and Simon? Aren't his sisters here with us?"

And they took offense at him. Jesus said to them, "***A prophet is not without honor except in his***

own town, among his relatives and in his own home." When prophesying to a people you know they make it their duty to scrutinize you based on their ideal and knowledge of your past, your genealogical association and even what you do for a living. The servants of God continue to face the same challenges today.

Jesus said that a prophet (in other words, a worker for God) is never honored in his hometown. But that does not make his work any less important. It is important that prophetic people are always aware that a person does not need to be respected or honored to be useful to God. If friends, neighbors or family do not respect your Christian work, do not allow their rejection to keep you from serving God. However, when the people you minister to is rebellious it will inhibit the expected outcome and limit your reach. Jesus could have done greater miracles in Nazareth, but he chose not to because of the people's pride and unbelief. The miracles he did had little effect on the people because they did not accept his message or believe that he was from God. Therefore, Jesus looked elsewhere, seeking those who would respond to His miracles and message.

In **Chapter Two,** when we examined how to grow in the prophetic, one such way was through a prophetic association or prophetic company. After Jesus was amazed at their lack of faith he went about teaching village to village. Jesus then sent the disciples two by two (or in pairs) and gave them authority over evil spirits. The disciples would have been from various locations and as such association or 'help' would have greatly reduced ineffectiveness from unbelieving people. Individually they could have reached more areas of the country, but this was not Jesus' plan. The advantages of going out by twos include the fact that they could encourage and strengthen each other.

Secondly, they could provide comfort in rejection and thirdly, they could give each other discernment, and fewer mistakes could be made. ***It is time Christians realize that our strength comes from God, but he meets many of our needs through our teamwork with others***. As you serve Christ, remember you cannot do it alone. Paul reminds us in Corinthians that we are all members of one body.

Many prophets or prophetic people tend to avoid grapevine, avoid passing judgments on people especially those they know and serve (their direct prophetic audience). This is important so that the flesh does not interfere with what God wants to convey to the people. When I am being used by God to prophesy especially in public, in my local church setting, I try to ensure that I listen carefully because, at no point, my knowledge of the person should influence what is communicated to or heard by the person to whom I am ministering. I try to follow the leading of the Spirit. I like when I am prophesying and it is accompanied by tongues because then, some of the 'embarrassing or sensitive information' is masked.

Another thing I try to practice is to ensure that I try to keep my mind as pure as is possible so that I am sensitive to the Spirit because not everything should be said via a microphone. There have been many instances where without thinking, the microphone is removed from my mouth and God would speak and people are receptive that way. However, this will not always be the case. The gift is to edify and correct, not to embarrass and kill.

Prophesying to a people you know can be intimidating or frightening, especially when you know well in advance the message you are expected to deliver. This can be extremely difficult if you are close to your people and it is a message of destruction. Jeremiah 1:17 recounts God giving his servant instruction. "Get yourself ready! Stand up and say to them whatever I command you. Do not be terrified by them, or I will terrify you before them. Today I have made you a fortified city, an iron pillar and a bronze wall to stand against the whole land—against the kings of Judah, its officials, its priests and the people of the land. They will fight against you but will not overcome you, for I am with you and will rescue you," declares the Lord. Jeremiah knew what he would face but He went in faith because God promised he would rescue him. God cautioned him not to be terrified or afraid or he will confound him before the people. This is serious, the message's delivery was hinged on Jeremiah's obedience. This warning was basically a repetition of this verse, "The righteous are as bold as a lion" (Prov. 28:1).

What I want you to take away from this subsection is that when God has given you a mandate, do it. When he has given you a word, release it (say it) without fear or favor because at the end of the day, if we faint, then our strength is small and this is contrary to the spirit that God has placed in us. His word tells us that "He has not given us a spirit of fear but of power, love and of a sound mind" (2 Tim. 1:7).

CHAPTER FIVE

Challenges of a Young Prophet

Throughout this book, many prophetic experiences throughout the Bible were cited. It was obvious that all prophets encountered challenges of some sort, some were even severe. Therefore, as a younger prophetic voice, it is even more challenging. If you recall in chapter one where we examined the levels of the prophetic, it is clear that a young prophet would have fewer experiences as 'young' in this case is not referring to age but rather one's prophetic journey.

Here are some challenges experienced by young prophets which I have also experienced:

Young prophets suffer *ridicule*. It is difficult to minister to people who are older than you in the faith. They are usually unwilling to obey and reluctant to hear what God is saying even if the word will save them from destruction. In some cases, it is usually when they have fallen in the ditch that a prophet's words are taken seriously.

The Bible speaks of the prophet's reward. This is something that I want us to acknowledge and be mindful of. Matthew 10:41-42 states: "Whoever welcomes a prophet as a prophet will receive a prophet's reward, and whoever welcomes a righteous person as a righteous person will receive a righteous person's reward. And if anyone gives even a cup of cold water to one of these little ones who is my disciple, truly I tell you, that person will certainly not lose their reward." I believe when you accept a prophet's instruction then you will be blessed, if it was a warning, you will be saved once you acknowledge and receive God's word through his servant. God regards his servants highly and as we have treated them, God will take note of it. Remember, the next time you hear a prophetic voice, ensure you discern the spirit because you do not want to mistreat one of God's. God takes note as if he were the one receiving it. Endeavour to entertain God.

While I am on this note, I am led to make an inference to the widow with the oil in 2 Kings 4:1-7 "The wife of a man from the company of the prophets cried out to Elisha, "Your servant my husband is dead, and you know that he revered the Lord. But now his creditor is coming to take my two boys as his slaves." Elisha replied to her, "How can I help you? Tell me, what do you have in your house?" "Your servant has nothing there at all," she said, "except a small jar of olive oil." Elisha said, "Go around and ask all your neighbors for empty jars. Don't ask for just a few. Then go inside and shut the door behind you and your sons. Pour oil into all the jars, and as each is filled, put it to one side." She left him and shut the door behind her and her sons. They brought the jars to her and she kept pouring. When all the jars were full, she said to her son, "Bring me another one." But he replied, "There is not a jar left". Then the oil stopped flowing. She went and told the man of God, and he said, "Go, sell the oil and pay your debts. You and your sons can live on what is left." The woman and her sons collected jars from their neighbours, pouring oil into them from their one pot. The oil was probably olive oil and was used for cooking, for lamps, and for fuel. The oil stopped pouring only when they ran out of containers. The number of jars gathered was an indication of their faith. God's provision was as large as their faith and willingness to obey. Beware of limiting God's blessings by a lack of faith and obedience. Be sure not to miss out on a prophet's reward.

Secondly, I am also impelled to cite the story of the Shunammite's son restored to life. One day Elisha went to Shunem. And a well-to-do woman was there, who urged him to stay for a meal. So whenever he came by, he stopped there to eat. She said to her husband, "I know that this man who often comes our way is a holy man of God. Let's make a small room on the roof and put in it a bed and a table, a chair and a lamp for him. Then he can stay there whenever he comes to us." One day when Elisha came, he went up to his room and lay down there. He said to his servant Gehazi, "Call the Shunammite". So he called her, and she stood before him. Elisha said to him, "Tell her,

'You have gone to all this trouble for us. Now, what can be done for you? Can we speak on your behalf to the king or the commander of the army?'" She replied, "I have a home among my own people."

"What can be done for her?" Elisha asked. Gehazi said, "She has no son, and her husband is old." Then Elisha said, "Call her." So he called her, and she stood in the doorway. "About this time next year," Elisha said, "you will hold a son in your arms." "No, my lord!" she objected. "Please, Man of God, don't mislead your servant!" But the woman became pregnant, and the next year about that same time she gave birth to a son, just as Elisha had told her. The child grew, and one day he went out to his father, who was with the reapers. He said to his father, "My head! My head!" His father told a servant, "Carry him to his mother." After the servant had lifted him up and carried him to his mother, the boy sat on her lap until noon, and then he died. She went up and laid him on the bed of the man of God, then shut the door and went out. She called her husband and said, "Please send me one of the servants and a donkey so I can go to the man of God quickly and return."

"Why go to him today?" he asked. "It's not the New Moon or the Sabbath." "That's all right," she said. She saddled the donkey and said to her servant, "Lead on; don't slow down for me unless I tell you." So she set out and came to the man of God at Mount Carmel. When he saw her in the distance, the man of God said to his servant Gehazi, "Look! There's the Shunammite! Run to meet her and ask her, 'Are you all right? Is your husband all right? Is your child all right?'" "Everything is all right," she said. When she reached the man of God at the mountain, she took hold of his feet. Gehazi came over to push

her away, but the man of God said, "Leave her alone!

She is in bitter distress, but the Lord has hidden it

from me and has not told me why." "Did I ask you for

a son, my lord?" she said. "Didn't I tell you, 'Don't

raise my hopes'?" Elisha said to Gehazi, "Tuck your

cloak into your belt, take my staff in your hand and

run. Don't greet anyone you meet, and if anyone

greets you, do not answer. Lay my staff on the boy's

face." But the child's mother said, "As surely as

the Lord lives and as you live, I will not leave you."

So he got up and followed her. Gehazi went on ahead

and laid the staff on the boy's face, but there was no

sound or response. So Gehazi went back to meet

Elisha and told him, "The boy has not awakened."

When Elisha reached the house, there was the boy

lying dead on his couch. He went in, shut the door on

the two of them and prayed to the Lord. Then he got on the bed and lay on the boy, mouth to mouth, eyes to eyes, hands to hands. As he stretched himself out on him, the boy's body grew warm. Elisha turned away and walked back and forth in the room and then got on the bed and stretched out on him once more. The boy sneezed seven times and opened his eyes. Elisha summoned Gehazi and said, "Call the Shunammite." And he did. When she came, he said, "Take your son." She came in, fell at his feet and bowed to the ground. Then she took her son and went out. I took you through this ordeal to see the depth and importance of a prophet's reward.

The Shunammite woman realized that Elisha was a man of God, and so she prepared a room for him to use whenever he was in town. She did this out of kindness and because she sensed a need, ***not for***

any selfish motives. Soon, however, her kindness would be rewarded gar beyond her wildest dreams. How sensitive are you to those who pass by your home and flow through your life-especially those preach and teach God's word? What special needs do they have that you could meet? As Christians, we need to do this self-evaluation regularly to ensure we are not missing out on the fullness of God.

Denial is another challenge faced by young prophets. People will refuse to believe that God has chosen you even when the signs are manifesting before their very eyes. Many young prophets are often rebuked especially when knowledge of the prophetic is not known in their locality. At the other end of the continuum, there may be those who deny and try to refute the fact that God needs prophets in this age-which he does. How do I know this?

According to Joel 2:28: "And afterward, I will pour out my Spirit on all people. Your sons and daughters will prophesy, your old men will dream dreams, your young men will see visions. And even if you fail to believe this, I am living in this truth. This is Another major reason why young prophets live in denial of the impending end which is here.

Many 'self-anointed, people-anointed, church-anointed prophets' are around. Because they might have discerned something accurately, they immediately think they are prophets. If the Lord has opened up their understanding to a dream or vision, they assume they are prophets without knowledge of the true prophetic anointing. Then, they end up being judgemental and even fanatics who tell people what their itching ears want to hear and wreak havoc in the kingdom of God.

Fear - Many young prophets like myself (even now writing this I am scared to use the title) because for me, it is something humbling, not anything to brag and boast about simply because it is not by my might nor by my power and also because the prophetic is so diverse and unpredictable and you can never be truly prepared for what God is about to do next.

Many other prophetic voices might be fearful for a number of reasons. Jonah, the prodigal prophet thought he could avoid God's call in his life by running away, by sacrificing himself, by belligerent obedience or even nullify God's call by sulking. Jonah's hatred was so strong that he did not want them to receive God's mercy (this was an enemy nation). Jonah was actually afraid the people would repent but there are some life lessons from Jonah's experience. God cares deeply for us as well as for people we resent and hate. God is patient with sinners and patient with his servants and finally, God will accomplish his purposes, even though reluctant and unwilling servants.

THE BIG QUESTION

What do I have the authority to prophesy?

As believers we all have the authority to prophesy using the Word of God. Therefore, you can prophesy to:

- yourself and your situation

&

- just about anything you are instructed to speak as you are led by the Spirit of God.

GLOSSARY

Definition of Technical Terms

A few specialized vocabulary you would have encountered in your read are defined just for you with reference to the Bible.

1. Affliction: great suffering that produces sorrow.

2. Anoint: to pour oil upon. It is usually used for healing or consecration to sacred duty; used for burial; figurative for divine appointment.

3. Antichrist: defined as the opponent of Christ as the prefix 'anti' means to oppose or against. The term is also used for the personification of evil (1 John 2: 18).

4. Apostle: means 'sent one'. Someone sent to represent another. In the New Testament someone who had seen Jesus and been commissioned by him to teach others about him.

5. Bless: to honour in worship; to offer approval or encouragement.

6. Blessing: refers to happiness; praise; divine favour or heavenly reward.

7. Prophecy: spoken or written communication from God, often but not always of a predictive nature. Message from a prophet (1 Cor. 14:1-5); Prophetess: a female prophet (Exodus 15:20).

8. Prophesy: to give a prophecy.

9. Prophet: one who gives a prophecy. A mouthpiece for God, one who receives a

message from God and proclaims it to a specific audience.

10. Vision: a supernatural revelation, message, or insight communicated through images seen only with a person's mind or spirit. The pictures seen in a vision may illustrate spiritual truths or future events. (Isaiah 1:1)

Isaiah 60

The future kingdom/The Glory of Zion

1"Arise, shine, for your light has come, and the

glory of the Lord rises upon you.

2 See, darkness covers the earth and thick darkness is

over the peoples, but the Lord rises upon you and his

glory appears over you.

3 Nations will come to your light, and kings to the

brightness of your dawn.

4 "Lift up your eyes and look about you: All

assemble and come to you; your sons come from afar,

and your daughters are carried on the hip.

5 Then you will look and be radiant, your heart will

throb and swell with joy; the wealth on the seas will

be brought to you, to you the riches of the nations

will come.

6 Herds of camels will cover your land, young camels of Midian and Ephah. And all from Sheba will come, bearing gold and incenseand proclaiming the praise of the Lord.

7 All Kedar's flocks will be gathered to you, the rams of Nebaioth will serve you; they will be accepted as offerings on my altar, and I will adorn my glorious temple.

8 "Who are these that fly along like clouds,

   like doves to their nests?

9 Surely the islands look to me; in the lead are the ships of Tarshish,[a] bringing your children from afar, with their silver and gold, to the honor of

the Lord your God,

the Holy One of Israel, for he has endowed you with splendor.

10 "Foreigners will rebuild your walls,

and their kings will serve you. Though in anger I

struck you, in favor I will show you compassion.

11 Your gates will always stand open,

they will never be shut, day or night,

so that people may bring you the wealth of the

nations—their kings led in triumphal procession.

12 For the nation or kingdom that will not serve you

will perish; it will be utterly ruined.

13 "The glory of Lebanon will come to you,

the juniper, the fir and the cypress together,

to adorn my sanctuary; and I will glorify the place for

my feet.

14 The children of your oppressors will come bowing

before you; all who despise you will bow down at

your feet and will call you the City of the Lord,

 Zion of the Holy One of Israel.

15 "Although you have been forsaken and hated,

   with no one traveling through, I will make you the

everlasting pride and the joy of all generations.

16 You will drink the milk of nations and be nursed at

royal breasts. Then you will know that I, the Lord, am

your Savior, your Redeemer, the Mighty One of

Jacob.

17 Instead of bronze I will bring you gold, and silver

in place of iron. Instead of wood I will bring you

bronze,

   and iron in place of stones. I will make peace your

governor and well-being your ruler.

18 No longer will violence be heard in your land,

   nor ruin or destruction within your borders,

but you will call your walls Salvation

and your gates Praise.

19 The sun will no more be your light by day,

nor will the brightness of the moon shine on you,

for the Lord will be your everlasting light,

and your God will be your glory.

20 Your sun will never set again,

and your moon will wane no more;

the Lord will be your everlasting light,

and your days of sorrow will end.

21 Then all your people will be righteous

and they will possess the land forever.

They are the shoot I have planted,

the work of my hands,

for the display of my splendor.

22 The least of you will become a thousand,

the smallest a mighty nation.

I am the Lord;

in its time I will do this swiftly."

75

When I first saw the design of this book's cover,

Isaiah 60 resonated with me.

SOME OF MY FAVOURITE BIBLE READS

We are to try and interact with all of scripture. That is God's expectation but these are some of my more frequent reads.

- Kings
- The book of Psalms – Psalm 3, 5, 6, 16, 19, 23, 24, 25, 26, 30, 32, 34, 36, 37, 52 among many others.
- The book of Proverbs (The entire book)
- The book of Jeremiah – Jer. 1, 16.
- Ezekiel- Eze. 1, 2, 18, 34, 37
- Daniel (The entire book)
- The Gospels - Matthew, Mark, Luke and John.
- Acts, and the remainder of the New Testament.

READING PLAN TO GET WISDOM

Wisdom is one of my heart's greatest desires. I keep memorizing Proverbs 2:12: "Wisdom will save you from the ways of the wicked men, from men whose ways are perverse". This is because I noticed that it is not how much we can jump, shout and roll for the Lord that will preserve us as saints, it is how much we have applied the Word of God to our daily walk. This is what will keep us.

The reading plan I want to share with you is simple. I developed the habit of reading **"a Proverb a day"**.

I started practicing this on a personal level from my first year in college. I recognized that the more I read it, the more I knew the Word. The more I knew, the more it resonated, and the more it resonated, the more I applied it. That was God! This is God's work, this is God's ideal for us. I believe this wholeheartedly because every wise person I know lives a victorious life through Christ Jesus.

How Does This Work?

Step 1: Get yourself a calendar

Step 2: Check to see the number of days in the month

Step 3: Get yourself a Bible (preferably a KJV and NIV)

Step 4: There are 31 chapters in Proverbs so read a chapter a day.

TIPS: Reading in the morning is better as it will chart the course of your day. In case you missed the morning read, read throughout the day or at night.

For months that have less than the 31 days, you can double up on any other day. Perhaps, one a day that resonates with you.

Step 5: In each chapter, highlight the verse that ministers to you most and ponder on it throughout the day. If needs be, you can note your interpretations.

TIPS: The book of Proverbs is very deep and has many themes and topics in one chapter. It takes a while to assimilate all of that knowledge into our spirits. Therefore, restarting the cycle/ reading plan each month helps in that regard.

At the end of each calendar year based on the month's noted assessment, you can tell whether or not you've achieved your goal.

ABOUT AUTHOR

Leroy Fearon is a humble young Christian who stands firm in his faith in Jesus Christ. He believes that God can do all things, not just a cliché but can do exceedingly abundantly all one can ask or imagine. He believes in big dreams and works assiduously to achieve them. Leroy is very active in ministry. He has preached on several occasions, also known to be an enthusiastic Bible teacher whom the Lord has blessed with an inimitable prophetic anointing.

Being blessed with many gifting and abilities, he is even more humbled and challenged knowing to whom much is given, much is expected. As a result, he has used his abilities to serve in areas such as Worship leader, Sunday teacher, preacher and usher in his local church body. He was appointed a little over two years ago as the National Youth Superintendent for his denomination in Jamaica. He was also a candidate to be installed as a Junior Pastor in his church.

The 24-year-old minister of the gospel is a high school teacher by profession. A teacher of the Humanities and Social Sciences with an emphasis in Geography. He is a punctilious worker and as such is extremely involved at school. At the work place, he has played several roles from emceeing numerous school events to sharing brief messages in devotions and being a part of two charity organisations. Achieved his Bachelor's degree with Honours at the age of 19 in one of the most challenging disciplines suggests that this young man was going places. His achievements did not end there. His most recent accomplishments include Assistant Examiner for CAPE Caribbean Studies; the Major examining body in the Caribbean, and he recently completed certification in Management from the University of the West Indies in December 2018 with emphasis on Supervisory Management. In addition, this book is even more recent of the recent, January 2019.

It is Leroy's desire that the end time church pay closer attention to the prophetic and what God is saying and doing in these last days. Hence the Lord inspired him to write this book, 'Learning the Prophetic' to better equip believers living in the end times and to keep them from being deceived from the many who will come in sheep's clothing claiming to be the Christ but inwardly they are ferocious wolves. He believes this book is a miracle as it was completed in record time-three days and it will minister to,

change perspectives and bless every reader's heart.

For consultation or comments, you may

contact the author at: leroyfearon85@gmail.com

NOTES

NOTES

NOTES

NOTES

NOTES